Drowning in the Drink

RADAR DEBOARD

"For all those battling addiction, we see you. You are not alone"

Chapter One

An unsettling notion drew Hailey from her slumber. As she drifted toward a more conscious state, a terrible sensation grew in her stomach. It was a feeling she had never experienced before, something that couldn't be put into proper words. She didn't even understand what was causing it. That didn't matter though because she knew one thing; that feeling was trying to warn her of something. It took a good minute of lying in the darkness, fighting the urge to simply close her eyes, for her to gain enough consciousness to sit up. In the pitch black that enveloped her, she sat and listened, waiting in fear for something to reach the room.

In the silence came dread, as her mind created the worst possible scenarios for why she had woken up. These thoughts filled her head in the unnaturally long minutes she sat in the dark. Finally, the sound of something foreign reached her ears. A disgusting squelching noise cut through the silence and confirmed a small part of her fear.

At the very least, something was amiss in her house. That thought was enough for Hailey to remove her feet from the sanctum under the thick comforter and place them oh-so-gently onto the carpeted floor. With as much meticulous effort as possible, she pulled the rest of her body from the bed while trying to minimize all noise.

She continued to listen to the sickening sound coming from somewhere in the dark, as she tentatively approached the wide-open door of her bedroom. Her hand came to rest on the light switch with a single finger held ready to flip it. A quick debate raged inside her brain before Hailey ultimately decided against using any lights. Instead, she stood peering into the suffocating black of her hallway, hoping that her eyes would adjust. When larger shapes began to appear in her field of vision, she decided that it would be fine to move forward. A right foot carefully broke the invisible barrier that separated her bedroom from the rest of the house, which meant there was no turning back.

The left foot slowly moved to meet its partner, carrying the grown woman who was plagued with fear. Hailey shuffled ever-so-slowly with cautious movements while the sensation of carpet rubbing against the soles of her feet accompanied her. After traveling only a few feet, she came to a stop before a closed door on her left. Gently, her hand reached out to grip the doorknob before turning it with a painstaking amount of effort. As she pushed it open, the door gave off a light squeak, and she froze. She held her breath, listening for any sounds of movement. She was met by only the uncomfortable squelching noise, which hadn't seemed affected by the creaking door.

She stood motionless for another minute or so before building the courage to push the door open just enough to peek inside. Her focus was immediately drawn to the small bed tucked in the left corner of the room. The night-light plugged into the adjacent wall shone enough light throughout the room that she could easily make out the shape of her young son sleeping soundly. Hailey kept her focus trained on him until she confirmed the rising and falling of his chest. With the knowledge that her child was safe, she softly shut the door before turning her attention back to the unnatural sound coming from somewhere in the house.

The second Hailey took a step back into the shrouded hallway, fear gripped at her stomach, squeezing the organ ever so tightly in its grasp. Despite the overwhelming urge to retreat into the bedroom, her motherly instincts prevented such action. Whatever was making the unsettling noise, she had to make sure it wouldn't do any harm to her or her child. Her tentative shuffling picked back up once more until she had exited several feet out of the corridor, and into the small living room, which put her just out of arm's reach of the kitchen.

Once again, she listened intently, desperately trying to pinpoint where the squelching originated from. It took but a few moments for her to rule out the kitchen; however, the living room was a different story. Being unable to eliminate the area where she currently stood caused Hailey's legs to shake from anxiety, but somehow, she managed to push herself forward. She quickly fell into a pattern of taking two steps before going completely motionless and checking how close she was to the squelching. After a few repetitions of this procedure, it became clear that the sound had to be coming from the compact basement. It was the last place she wanted to go in the middle of the night.

Each step became an internal battle, but eventually, she reached the stairs. Hailey tried to peer down the steps, though utter darkness prevented her vision from making it more than a few feet. In anticipation of the descent, she took in a long, uneven breath of air. With the oxygen held in her lungs, she took that first hesitant step down with her toes, feeling to make sure there was something solid waiting for them.

Hailey's focus was placed so heavily on simply moving down the steps that she wasn't paying attention to the squelching sound for several precious seconds. In that amount of time, the noise rapidly progressed toward her, becoming loud enough that she picked up on it once again. She froze in terror as the grotesque sound from the dark sped forward, her body failing to retreat or react. It was too late when she realized the squelching had stopped just off to her right.

Gripped by a sudden panic, she whipped her head toward the wall just a few feet from her face. The squelching stopped for a moment only to be replaced with an alien-like squeal. A second later something wet and sticky slapped onto the side of her face. Taken by surprise, Hailey took a step forward, only for her left foot to touch nothing but air. She hung there for a moment before momentum and gravity brought her falling downward. Her body couldn't react quickly enough and she tumbled down the narrow stairwell, limbs slamming against the railing and sidewall as she went.

The fall ended with her landing in the basement, the thinly carpeted floor doing little to mitigate the damage of the concrete. She landed headfirst, sending an eruption of pain spreading through the back of her skull. Her body twitched and spasmed as she lay there in agony, completely forgetting about the foreign substance that had attached itself to her cheek. That is, until the strange and slimy thing began to crawl over her face. Hailey let out a terror-filled gasp as she tried to rip the unnatural material off, but her arms completely failed her.

Desperately, she tried to move any part of her body, but the pain was too great. She felt the slimy substance crawl to the edge of her mouth and time froze for a moment. There was a second or two where the gunk seemed like it would just stop, but then it slipped into her open mouth. From there she could feel it force its way upward inside her head. The agony of the creature forcing its way up through her sinuses mixed with the pain from the fall nearly caused Hailey's mind to go blank. After minutes spent in agony, she felt the thing somehow break itself into her skull and crawl over her brain. That's when she started to drift in and out of consciousness as a new sound barely reached her ears. The familiar noise of little footsteps moving slowly over carpet, kept her holding on.

"Mommy?" her precious son called out from the top of the steps.

Hailey tried to reply, but a weak gasp was the only sound that escaped her lips. Even as her son began to cautiously head down the steps, she couldn't stay awake. With her eyes closing, she heard the worry in her son's voice as he called out once more, "Mommy?"

Chapter Two
Five months since infection

THE DINER WAS PACKED, at least by its standards. Roughly two-thirds of the seats were taken, which led to an overwhelmed staff. Even though she had been waitressing for well over a decade, rushes still managed to get under Hailey's skin. Maybe it was because the clientele was predominately made up of the grouchy elderly. Folks that took forever to decide what they wanted, along with being horrific tippers and generally less patient than younger customers. It didn't take much to send an ancient hag into a yelling fit. Giving an old bat three pieces of bacon instead of four would have any of them screaming their lungs out.

This was the unfortunate situation that Hailey faced after already putting in a full eight hours on the night shift. The latter half of her double was certainly turning into something that came straight out of hell. Yet, she pushed her way through all the indecisive and grouchy guests while somehow not losing her cool. All of that changed roughly an hour before noon, because that was when the whispers started up. A cacophony of quiet voices joined to create an amalgamation that she couldn't understand and only worked to grow her already rising agitation.

Forcing the best smile possible given the situation, she continued to power through her shift. As the minutes ticked by, the whispers gradually grew louder inside her mind, drowning out the usual sounds of a shift. The customer's orders all slurred together once they reached her ears while the noises of tickets being ready and dishes clacking together were completely overpowered. Hailey's thoughts were in complete chaos well before the end of her shift. When the time finally came for her to clock out, there were no additional moments spent lingering inside the diner. She booked it out the door without even saying goodbye to her coworkers.

The whispers continued to assail her brain as she sped her car out of the parking lot and headed for the highway. It had been months now since her fall down the stairs. Dozens of weeks spent with injuries because she couldn't afford a trip to the hospital. More importantly, it had been months since something crawled inside her mouth and wiggled its way into her brain. Hailey knew that whatever had gotten in that night was precisely what was causing the whispers. Unfortunately, she had no idea how to get it out of her head. However, she knew exactly what to do to calm the voices, how to keep them at bay ... at least for a little bit.

The temporary cure for her problem waited at home, which left her all too eager to speed down the highway, weaving in and out of traffic. She made it in record time and dashed to the door of the homely duplex. A sudden screech came from the voices as Hailey tried to unlock the front door and almost fumbled the keys from her grasp. Desperation to be rid of the whispers gave way to erratic movements, to the point where she nearly forced the lock. Thankfully, it didn't come to that, but she did throw the door wide open, its knob slamming against the wall and creating a scuff mark.

She completely ignored the damage, leaving the entrance to her house wide open while hustling into the kitchen. Her hand wrapped around the handle for the top cabinet, nearly out of her reach. She pulled it open before ramming her fingers into the open space to blindly search for the large plastic bottle that was up there. After a few stumbling moments, she felt a smooth surface not composed of wood, and her fingers wrapped around it. A small gasp of exertion came from her lips as she brought the bottle of coconut rum down to eye level. Without a second thought, she twisted off the cap and downed a good gulp or two of the liquor. Almost immediately she coughed at the unpleasant taste, but fought through it to take another decent-sized drink.

Once the foul liquid had slid its way down her throat, she stood still with closed eyes while the whispers continued. After several drawn-out moments, the volume of the voices decreased by the tiniest amount. Hailey took another swig and waited for the cacophony inside her mind to grow quiet before letting out a deep sigh. Though the whispers continued their ramblings, they were soft enough that she could actually think. She put the bottle away before finally shutting the front door of the duplex. From there she made her way over to the couch and plopped down on it, while letting out a long sigh. She was thankful that Michael was still at school and hadn't stumbled upon her in such a desperate state.

"It's only to stop the whispers," she told herself. "That's all it is."

Chapter Three
One to nine years since infection

Hailey was so tired of having to deal with the constant strain on her psyche. The annoying little voices filled her head with their unintelligible ramblings. It took most of her mental energy just to hear others talk when the internal ensemble blabbered away. The one solace came from alcohol. It was the only thing that kept it at bay and lessened the attacks on her mind. She had gone to several different psychologists and tried various antipsychotics, but none of it worked. Even dabbling in Eastern medicine did nothing to assuage the situation. So, she had turned to the only thing that brought her any relief.

At first, it had just been coconut rum, the only kind of liquor that she could tolerate the taste of. On top of that, she would only take a few drinks from the bottle, and that never happened more than once or twice a day. Eventually, the voices seemed to grow an immunity to the tactic. Hailey had to partake in larger portions at a time, returning to the bottle more frequently with each passing day. Soon, she had to start mixing it with soda, pouring a half rum, half pop concoction. Again, it worked for a little while, but the whispers came back even more overwhelming than before.

Despite the constant assaults on her brain, she tried to keep going through her day-to-day like nothing was wrong. Hailey had enough experience as a waitress that she was able to make it through most workdays while heavily relying on her instincts and experience. More often than not, this led to excruciating headaches due to the voices' constant attacks. She pushed through the pain, unaided during work, for several months until she realized that coconut rum looked a hell of a lot like water. Once that epiphany had hit her, she was using a little liquid courage cut with water for every one of her shifts. Thanks to muscle memory and her years of work at the diner, she was able to navigate the floor even while being a bit tipsy.

Though she was able to keep her professional life intact, it was her personal one that suffered. Due to the constant berating of the whispers, Hailey found it difficult to keep track of the parts of life that weren't part of her recurring schedule. This wasn't too much of a problem in the beginning as her son didn't have a lot of friends, and still wasn't old enough for extracurricular activities. He needed to be dropped off and picked up at the same time five days a week, which was easy for her to keep track of. However, once he became interested in basketball, that whole schedule was thrown out the window.

She tried to keep track of the new routine, but the coach decided it would be best to alternate practice days. Thanks to the shake-up, as well as her self-medication against the whispers, Hailey ended up being late picking him up from practice. She was only thirty minutes late, but with the distinct smell of alcohol on her breath, that was enough to sow distrust from the other adults. All and all, she ended up only being late one other time to pick him up during that first season of basketball. Yet, the smell of rum clung to her, and the coach took note of it.

At the same time she was trying to stay a good mother, the whispers seemingly became immune to her drink of choice. This led to Hailey moving on to harder liquor, stuff that was at least seventy-proof. She graduated to two shots of tequila mixed with orange juice for several months before having to up the alcohol content from there. After a few months of that, her tolerance was too high, and she had to start adding dashes of 100-proof vodka to all her drinks that weren't water. Each time she upped the amount of alcohol she took in; it kept the voices at bay for just a little while. They seemed to grow stronger with time, and a hint of anger seeped into their tone. They had become more aggressive when they assailed her, hitting her at all hours of the night.

The late-night ramblings made it impossible for Hailey to get a good night's sleep. This further impaired her thinking and left her brain even worse off than it already was. Regardless, she kept trying to push through everything and fool everyone into thinking she was doing okay. Her ruse worked for another year or two, but it quickly fell apart when she missed her son's fifth-grade graduation. That's when the rumors started to swirl among the other parents, and eventually reached the ears of their children. Soon her son was ridiculed at school for having an alcoholic bum for a mom. All the bullying hurt her son, and he became more withdrawn and isolated from Hailey.

It soon became clear to her that her own child wanted to avoid her. Though she didn't know the reason why, regardless, it hurt her all the same. This emotional pain led to her starting to consume more alcohol just before bed, sometimes staying up until she had a good buzz going. Eventually, Hailey began putting straight vodka in her bottles and passing it off as water. She managed to bluff her way through work while being full-on drunk for almost every shift. Of course, that eventually came back to bite her in the butt when she slipped and injured her back while carrying two arms full of customers' food. In a stroke of incredible luck, all who had witnessed the incident pointed to a wet floor being the culprit, while no one even suspected she had been tossed three sheets to the wind. Thanks to her injury due to "unsafe working conditions", Hailey was able to receive a nice payout from the courts.

The money was supposed to help with her medical bills and be supplemental income until she could get back to work, but that didn't happen. Instead, Hailey ended up using the payout to buy booze. With nothing but time on her hands during the day, the voices grew more intense, and in turn, she drank more. Her consumption doubled, reaching a point where she was smashed for every waking moment. All that alcohol eventually resulted in a sudden drop in blood sugar and her passing out in the middle of the living room. Once again, for the second time in his life, her son was witness to the scarring scene of his mother lying unconscious on the floor, with him having no idea if she would wake up. So, he did the only thing he could; with tears running down his cheeks, he called an ambulance.

The doctor had been a straight shooter with her, either she stopped hitting the bottle or she would end up in an early grave. Of course, they didn't know about the whispers tearing at the seams of her sanity. Alcohol was the only thing that kept her from turning into a raving lunatic, at least, that's what she told herself. Ultimately, she kept drinking while the voices grew stronger and her body grew weaker.

Through all of it, she continued to forget or completely miss important milestones of her child. During the first two years of his high school basketball career, she only managed to make it to one game, and she was blackout drunk for it. Worst of all, he could hear her getting plastered every night. It took him hours of pretending that he couldn't hear Hailey mixing drinks before he would be able to fall asleep. Then, long after initially falling asleep, her staggering down the hallway would always manage to wake him up. Gradually, the pain and grief he felt for what his mother was becoming morphed into anger, which further grew into hatred. There was only so much hurt that he could take while keeping his mouth shut. Eventually, his rage boiled over and he confronted his mother.

"Why do you keep doing this?" he yelled, demanding a response.

Unfortunately, at the time, Hailey was already on her fourth mixture of vodka combined with whatever juice was still left in the fridge. Her mind took a few seconds longer than usual to process the rage-filled question her son had levied toward her. "W-What do you mean, baby?" she managed to get out while only lightly slurring the words together.

"It's a weeknight, Mom! Why are you drinking?"

"Oh, you mean this?" she chuckled while raising the coffee mug containing her spiked beverage. "This is nothing, honey…j-just a little something to take off the edge."

Despite her best judgment, Hailey had brought the mug up to her lips and taken a loud sip of the concoction, enraging her son. Without another word, her child stormed off to his room, slamming the door shut and leaving her alone in the living room. That was his breaking point, and their relationship completely deteriorated. Of course, Hailey had no way of knowing that at the time. There were only two things she was aware of in the moment: the nice numbing feeling that washed through her body, and the fact that the whispers were so quiet she could barely hear them. So, instead of stumbling down the hall to try to fix things with her son, she sat there, drinking alone.

Chapter Four
Thirteen years since infection

A SERIES OF WET coughs forcing their way out from Hailey's dry throat pulled her to a half-conscious state. She hacked up a chunk of phlegm with the clump of mucus shooting out from her mouth and onto her thick comforter. After several seconds of stillness, she finally rubbed her eyes while letting out a loud groan. She completely ignored the glob of snot sitting beside her and instead put her efforts into sitting up, while a grunt escaped her mouth due to the amount of exertion placed on the simple task. Once sitting upright, her eyes fought desperately to adjust to the small sliver of light that showed through the crack in her curtains.

After staring off for several minutes, she finally stumbled out of bed. Her underutilized legs struggled to carry the weight placed on them and she nearly fell straight into the wall. Hailey just barely managed to keep that from happening by extending her arm in the nick of time. Another set of vicious coughs sprang forth from her throat, which forced the woman, who was a shell of her former self, to lean against the wall for support. It took far longer than she wanted to for the fit to finally cease, the coughs being so violent that they left her hands shaking. After taking a moment to catch her breath, she noticed a warm sensation coming from her right leg. A glance down and she spotted the clear wet spot running down the inside of the left leg of her grey sweatpants.

"Damnit, not again," she mumbled under her breath.

Hailey glared at the dark spot on her pants for well over a minute before finally heading toward the bathroom. It took a few steps for her to get her balance, though she continued to brace herself against the wall all the way to her destination. She passed through the wide-open door to the bathroom and was immediately greeted by the pungent smell of vomit. Normally, she wasn't bothered by the horrific odors that lurked about her house, but the one that assaulted her nostrils was so bad that it caused her to gag. She only lasted a few seconds with the smell before she instinctively went for the sink, letting a wave of bile rocket up from her throat.

Unpleasant noises escaped from her as discolored liquid spilled forth into the sink. Thanks to not having consumed much food over the past few days, there were no chunks of unidentifiable substances in the vomit; it was just a runny concoction that flew out. The new bile landed on top of an older set of throw-up, slipping through the small cracks in the dried refuse to thankfully spill into the drain. Hailey took in a few sharp gasps before another grouping of vomit forced its way up her esophagus. She heaved the unpleasant material out with a horrific gagging sound. The energy expended on the whole ordeal quickly sent her to her knees, desperately gasping for air.

As she sat there trying to recover from the ordeal, a slight noise began to fill her head. It only took a few moments after that for the whispers to creep into her mind. Despair immediately gripped her while the familiar voices gradually grew in volume. She barely had any respite from the constant sounds that plagued her sanity. For years she had been subjected to their nearly unending barrages, which drove her closer to the brink. With each passing day, she could feel her will growing weaker to their onslaughts. Though there was no way to decipher what the voices were saying, she could guess from their tones. Their ultimate goal was to bring about her end, and they were pushing her ever closer to it.

Suddenly overwhelmed by the noise inside her brain, Hailey furiously beat the sides of her head with her open hands. "Shut up! Shut up! Shut up!"

Taken over by an intense fury, Hailey stumbled to her feet and hurried down the hall while continuing to beat the sides of her skull. Precious seconds passed before she reached the kitchen, the voices growing ever louder with each step. Frantically, she threw open the cabinets, searching with frenzied energy for the one thing that could alleviate her predicament. After knocking over everything on a dozen shelves, she finally came across a half-empty bottle of scotch behind several bags of chips. Haphazardly, she ripped the scotch from its resting place near the back of the shelf, flinging various items of junk food onto the floor in the process.

She paid no attention to the mess she made and cracked open the liquor, inhaling a massive gulp of the amber-colored beverage. When there was no immediate relief to the cacophony that assailed her mind, she tipped the drink up and allowed the contents of the bottle to run over her tongue and down her throat. The wave of scotch quickly caused a burning sensation and in reaction to it, Hailey instinctively tried to suck in a breath, causing liquor to go down the wrong pipe. Immediately, she began a fit of violent hacking as her body tried to expel the liquid from where it wasn't supposed to be.

The fitful coughs continued for well over a minute, sapping a great deal of energy from Hailey. As the situation finally calmed, she pressed her back against a set of cabinets and slowly sank to the floor. She sat for a few minutes as the alcohol slowly took effect and the voices grew back into whispers. Not content with the lingering sounds, she took another deep gulp from the bottle before pulling herself off the floor. Without trying to clean up any of the random items strewn about the kitchen, she slowly shuffled into the hallway and headed back to the bedroom. As she moved along, she would periodically take a few sips of the scotch.

By the time she collapsed into bed, there was a little under a quarter of the bottle left and she intended to take care of it quickly. A few minutes later and the scotch was all but drained, which in turn silenced the whispers for some much-needed respite. Hailey tossed the bottle onto the floor as she pulled the large comforter up to her neck. Despite being up for an hour tops, she was already feeling completely drained. She had no will to do anything productive, as the prospect of the voices emerging while she was in the middle of doing something was too much for her to handle. Instead, she simply closed her eyes as the familiar and warm feeling of inebriation washed over her.

Chapter Five
Two days since infection succeeding

Michael turned his beat-up car onto the residential street as the tire pressure light flashed. Just like the check engine light that had been perpetually on for well over six months, he decided to ignore the warning. His car was a piece of crap; he would be the first to say it. A tail-light was out and the vehicle itself had well over two hundred thousand miles on it. There was no point in replacing anything major as he was just going to get a new one in a year or two. Even if he wanted to fix the vehicle, he didn't have the money to do so.

As he slowly drove through the neighborhood, he observed that the condition of his car matched the area. Nearly every house he saw was rundown or headed in that direction thanks to neglect. It wasn't a very savory area of town, but there was a reason he had come there. Michael made his way past a few more rough-looking houses before coming to a stop in front of a small home with chipped blue paint covering the outside of it. He took a deep breath to ready himself before exiting the vehicle and reluctantly trudging up the tiny driveway.

After knocking a few times he called out, "Mom! Are you in there?"

Several moments passed with no response, so he rapped his knuckles against the door. When he was met by silence once more, Michael let out a deep sigh and turned away from the house for a moment. He scanned the street, taking note of the random bits of furniture and equipment that littered people's yards. The outdated houses overgrown with weeds did not make him feel safe and he turned his attention back to his mother's place. He knocked once again but quickly grew impatient, proceeding to bang his fist against the wood of the door.

"Mom, come on!" he yelled. His anger began to rise, and after a few seconds, he shouted, "It's two in the afternoon! Are you seriously not awake?"

Yet again, Michael was met by silence. He stood there for a long minute before trying the doorknob as a last measure before leaving. To his surprise, the door was unlocked and easily opened for him. This didn't sit right with him, especially considering that break-ins happened quite often in that part of town. Worry started to bubble in his gut as he tentatively stepped into the house. He stood just inside the doorway for a minute, gathering his courage, then progressed into the living room. The first thing he noticed was the remains of several microwaved dinners left on a coffee table that was also littered with candy wrappers. Knowing his mom, this was nothing out of the ordinary, but it didn't put his mind at ease.

He moved over to the coffee table to get a closer look, noticing the various stains spread throughout the carpet as he went. Once he was standing over the pile of decimated plastic trays, an unpleasant odor wafted up to his nostrils. He instinctively crinkled his nose in disgust and tried to locate the cause of the stench. His focus became concentrated on patches of fuzzy white and blue chunks that lingered inside the frozen dinner containers. The sight of what was clearly mold combined with the smell caused him to gag and quickly backtrack a few feet.

Michael turned his head away from the mess and toward the recliner that sat a few feet from him. Once again, he was met by a foul odor that curiosity drove him to investigate. It took one glance for him to spot the large piss stain that covered the seat of the chair. Clearly his mother had failed to make it to the bathroom on more than one occasion, no doubt thanks to the copious amounts of alcohol she had been guzzling. He moved away from the urine-stained furniture and pivoted his attention to the kitchen. The sheer amount of items that littered the floor and countertops was astonishing. Various perishable and nonperishable goods were spilled about the area, which brought the idea of a robbery back to the forefront of his mind.

From what he had seen so far, he was very reluctant to search the rest of the property, but part of him was determined to continue. So, he trekked from the kitchen to the one hallway in the house and proceeded to move down it with extreme caution. Part of him didn't want to believe that his mom created such a mess on her own, but that would have meant someone else had done it, and that possibility was worse. Michael couldn't think of a reason why anyone would believe his mom had money. There was no way to know that based on what she owned. Her house, her car, even her clothes were all rundown and old. Yet, she did have money from her sizable work-related settlement from a few years prior.

"Maybe she told one of her dumb friends about it," Michael mumbled to himself as he came to a stop in front of the first closed door he encountered.

Deciding to be extra cautious, he placed an ear against the door to listen for any sounds coming from the other side. After hearing nothing, he decided it was safe enough to enter, though he was still hesitant to continue. His heartbeat picked up as he gripped the knob and warily pushed open the door inch by inch. He kept expecting something to pop out or for someone to be waiting and attack him, but nothing happened. Instead of coming face to face with a loaded gun, as he feared, Michael was met with his old room. Everything seemed to be in order as he scanned the area. In fact, his mom had left all his stuff exactly as it had been the day he left for college. Though he occasionally dropped by to check on his mother, he never spent any real time in her house. This was the farthest he had gone inside in over two years.

It was surreal to see his old room in such pristine condition compared to the rest of the house. To him, that was telling of his mom's mindset. She was completely okay with trashing everything that belonged to her but didn't want to mess up anything of his. His mom wanted to keep his room safe from the reckless behavior she participated in. He didn't know why, but it caused him to choke up a bit. She cared enough to keep his stuff from becoming contaminated by her drinking. If she had only done the same thing for him, maybe he wouldn't have felt the need to escape. Perhaps he would have come and visited her more often. Regardless, Michael wasn't leaving until he made sure his mother was okay.

He stepped back into the hallway, making sure to close the door behind him before continuing. After taking only a few steps, he was yet again hit by a pungent odor, this one coming from the bathroom. He plugged his nose with his fingers and entered to find that a huge puddle of vomit clogging the sink was the culprit. Thanks to the makeshift plug made of bile, the smell was so strong that still it managed to slip into his nostrils, nearly causing him to retch. For the second time in a few minutes, he had to frantically backtrack out of an area due to the stench alone. Michael threw caution to the wind as he exited the bathroom, slamming the door behind him.

He took a few moments to recover in the hallway, not even registering what he had done until the lingering odor cleared from his sinuses. Once he was hit with the realization of the noise he had made, a bundle of dread slammed into his gut. An uneasy sensation washed over him as he anxiously waited to see if anyone wishing to do him harm would emerge from an uninspected area of the house, but no one came. He was left with silence and a growing comprehension that there was only one room left he hadn't searched yet. All the signs littered across the house did not lend credence to his theory of a break-in, but Michael didn't want to admit that to himself. He turned his attention to the back bedroom while taking the slowest steps he could muster, to allow as much time as possible before he reached the truth.

"Mom?" he called out weakly as he placed a hand against the wall for support. "A-Are you awake?"

Michael knew there wasn't going to be an answer. Long before he physically reached the door, he knew what awaited him inside. His gut told him not to enter, but he refused to listen to it and crossed through the doorway. He still didn't rely on his intuition even as he stared at his mom lying completely still, face up in bed. The unnatural purple tone of her skin combined with the smell of feces didn't convince him of the truth. It wasn't until he was directly next to her, gently touching the icy, cold skin of her arm that it finally dawned on him. In an instant, the world seemed to fall directly on top of him, crushing his spirit under its weight.

"Wake up!" he suddenly shouted. Desperation took over and he tried shaking his mother awake while repeatedly screaming, "Don't do this to me!"

He shook the lifeless body until he finally processed the reality of the situation. That's when the grief slammed into him at full force, and the tears immediately started to flow. There was so much pain in the moment he couldn't think straight. He just stood there weeping while looking down at the lifeless body of his mother, the only family he had ever known. It was too much for him to handle. All he could do was stand there; his eyes scanned her corpse until they came to rest on an anomaly just below her nose. There appeared to be a strange, black substance that had run out of her nostrils at some point before, or possibly after her death. It was a peculiar detail that sparked Michael's curiosity. A brief break in the overwhelming grief came as he leaned over his mother's lifeless frame to get a better look at the mysterious substance.

"What in the ..." he began to say as the black material started to bubble.

Before he could finish speaking, the foreign gunk suddenly jumped off his mother and landed with a splat on the right side of his face. Michael let out a yelp of surprise and fell backward onto the floor. He scrambled to his feet and took off out of the bedroom as the strange material started to crawl its way across his face. Thinking quickly, he rushed into the bathroom, adrenaline kicking in, allowing him to disregard the pungent odor that filled the area. He stared into the mirror just in time to spot the black substance moving toward his eye. Instinctively he slapped his hand onto the entity in an attempt to crush it.

A wet splat sounded, and he assumed that he had taken care of it, but that wasn't the case. A few seconds later, the material slipped through his fingers and successfully reached his eye. Michael let out a terror-filled scream as the gunk pushed itself under his eyelid and past the actual organ. Agony burst forth from the entity's entry point in his body, and he collapsed to the floor. Mere moments passed before the unbearable pain pushed upward toward his skull, and he screamed even louder as he clutched the top of his head. A quick sting of agony hit his brain in an instant, and then the pain started to subside. Meanwhile, his brain felt as though it had been placed into a fog while the energy rapidly drained from him. Michael fought against the overwhelming urge to sleep, but he lost the battle, falling unconscious on the disgusting bathroom floor.

Chapter Six
Eleven months since infection

THE ICY WIND SMACKED against Michael's face, stinging his skin. He readjusted the hood of his jacket, trying to gain some protection from the elements, but it was no use. The inclement weather was too powerful, and the cold seeped through his clothes. His skin hurt with each bit of movement, but he pushed forward over the sidewalk that had become slippery from the sleet that started coming down when he first began his trek. Despite his overwhelming desire to drive, he knew that wasn't a smart choice, not with the nice buzz he'd gotten from finishing off the last of his bourbon.

So, he desperately tried to hold on to the pleasant, warming sensation from the alcohol as he pushed forward through the awful elements. The sleet rapidly picked up, and his face quickly became numb from the tiny chunks of ice that slapped against it. Michael let out a gasp of pain as his left foot stepped into a small puddle of icy water. That unpleasant sensation kickstarted a spark of adrenaline, and he picked up the pace into a slow jog while his hands remained stuffed in his jacket pockets. His lungs started to burn after only a minute or so; with each breath the frigid air stung his insides. Finally, he reached his destination, frantically throwing open the door before rushing inside.

"Jesus Christ, Michael! What the hell are you doing walking in this weather?" the on-duty employee asked from his spot behind the bar.

Michael took his sweet time moving from the door over to the nearest stool, gasping for air as he sat. "You know me ... I like a challenge."

The bartender scoffed before setting a paper coaster down in front of the new arrival. "Well ... what'll it be?"

After taking a quick scan of all the liquor covering the shelves before him, Michael replied, "I'll take a whiskey sour."

With a simple nod, the bartender went about creating the cocktail as Michael pulled his jacket hood off. He removed his hands from the insulated pockets, pain flowing through them as cold cracked the skin. Somewhat concerned for his digits, he tried rubbing the clenched fingers of one hand against the palm of the other. The generated friction helped a tiny bit, but there was no doubt his appendages would remain in glacial pain for a good ten or fifteen minutes. Regardless, he continued his pathetic attempt to create some body heat as he glanced around the bar. It was nearly empty except for a grouping of rough customers in a back corner and a sprinkling of couples here and there.

His people-watching was interrupted by the sound of glass being set down upon the bar. He turned to find his whiskey sour ready for enjoyment. Immediately, he forgot about the frigid pain in his hands and picked up the cold beverage. After knocking back a good portion of the drink in a single go, he placed the half-empty glass down on the dirty bar and signaled to the bartender for another. Michael didn't waste any time and downed the rest of the beverage, letting out a loud sigh of pleasure after doing so. While he waited on his refill, he braved a handful of bar peanuts. The snack had been there for quite some time, as he could taste the staleness of them, but he hadn't eaten in over twelve hours so he happily ate the makeshift meal. The bartender wordlessly placed the new drink down next to the empty one, and Michael eagerly took it in hand.

He waited until after swallowing the collection of peanuts he had been munching on, before raising the glass and muttering cheers to no one in particular. Using a bit more restraint than before, he only took a sip from the whiskey sour as he turned to find a new place to sit and nurse his drink. There was a booth near the back that happened to be partially bathed in shadow, which suited Michael. He stood up from the barstool and was hit by the first whiskey sour, restoring the buzz from earlier. With a pleasant feeling flowing through him, he absentmindedly started walking while his focus remained on the booth. As he went to take another sip of his drink, someone lightly bumped into his left side, causing him to spill some of the drink over himself.

"What the hell?" he snapped while turning to identify the culprit.

A woman, probably only a few years older than him, met his gaze. Based on her appearance and attire, Michael would have normally assumed she was a college student, but the fact that she was in the same bar as him all but eliminated that possibility. There was a clear glaze in her eyes, which showed she had been more successful at getting drunk than him that evening. He broke eye contact with the perpetrator to assess his drink, finding that over a quarter of it had been spilled over his coat.

"Watch where you're going," the woman snapped.

Michael pivoted his focus to the lady while letting out in an agitated tone, "Excuse me?"

"Watch where you're going, asshole."

"Me? Lady, you're the one who bumped into me."

The woman rolled her eyes as she took a step to maneuver around him, "Whatever."

Michael wanted to follow her to continue the confrontation, but his exhaustion convinced him not to. Instead, he finished the advance toward his chosen booth while muttering, "Stupid bitch."

He slid into the open seat while taking care not to spill any more of his drink. Michael scooted across the seat until he was against the wall, half concealed in shadow. From his somewhat hidden spot, he nursed his whiskey sour while scanning the other patrons. Bits of laughter broke through the classic rock blasting over the speakers. The happiness annoyed him, but ultimately it didn't really matter as the faintest of whispers continued to peck at his mind. He knew it would take at least two more drinks before they completely faded for a bit, but at the moment, he wanted to enjoy the cocktail in his hands. So, Michael took small sips as he sat alone in his grief and woe.

Chapter Seven
One year since infection

He slammed the glass down a little too hard on the table, and it slipped out of his grasp. Thankfully, he had just downed his drink, otherwise, there would have been a much larger mess when it tipped over. Ice still spilled out onto the smooth surface, and Michael grunted in annoyance as he grabbed a few napkins and tossed them on top of the small spill. He leaned back, allowing himself to rest his body against the seat while commencing a long session of staring into space. By some significant amount of luck, it only took three rum and cokes to quiet the whispers to where he could actually think.

Some time to reflect on things was exactly what Michael needed. After all, it had almost been a year to the day since stumbling upon his mother. The whole ordeal still haunted him; he saw her pale, lifeless face nearly every time he closed his eyes. It had truly been an unrelenting year filled with depression, wherein he made next to no progress in moving on. How could he? Especially since he had a reminder of that day relentlessly nagging at him inside his head. The damn voices constantly drove him to drink, which was the reason he flunked out of his last semester of college, along with losing the part-time job at the local credit union.

There was one good thing that did come out of the shit sandwich of a year ... he started to understand what his mom had gone through. If she had been infected with the same black gunk as him, then it made sense why she became a belligerent drunk. Of course, this revelation also added to his guilt, seeing as he abandoned his mother in her time of need. And considering that it really wasn't her fault she was drinking, it only made it that much worse. Michael was just about to pull himself out of the booth to get another drink to drown his sorrow and guilt in when someone came to a stop in a spot where he couldn't exit the seat. He looked up to see the woman who had bumped into him a few days ago. It took him a couple of seconds to process who she was, but once he had, he let out an audible sigh.

"Fuck me," he grumbled under his breath. Michael inhaled deeply before bluntly asking, "What do you want?"

The woman silently stood there, looking a tad uncomfortable. She hesitated a few moments longer until she quickly blurted out, "I'm sorry."

Michael blinked a few times before letting out a guttural, "Huh?" in response.

"I'm sorry about the other day. I was having a bad time and ..."

"What are you talking about?" Michael asked in confusion.

"I bumped into you, you moron!" she snapped. The woman shook her head before saying in a much calmer tone, "What I'm saying is ... I'm sorry I made you spill your drink the other night."

"Um...thanks...I guess," Michael slowly replied, somewhat confused.

She nodded, pursing her lips before continuing, "Let me make it up to you. Let me get your next drink. What are you having?"

Michael glanced at his tipped-over glass, thinking heavily about whether he wanted this random lady to buy him a drink. After a few moments, his want for more booze won out and he replied, "I guess I'll take a gin and tonic."

"Okie dokie. Gimmie a few, and I'll be right back," she said with a wink before walking off.

He skeptically watched out of the corner of his eye as the strange woman made her way to the bar. In all honesty, he didn't expect her to return with a drink for him, and that was perfectly fine. All he wanted was some time to think about the unfortunate anniversary that loomed over him. His mind filtered out all except for the image of his mother's still face, lifeless and drained of nearly all its color. He kept it as the only thing floating in his brain, holding on to it like some sort of punishment for not being there to save her. Michael's grief and self-loathing grew as he sat in the empty booth, so absorbed by the emotions that he hardly registered the drink being placed right in front of him.

With a gesture of her hand, the woman announced, "There you are. A gin and tonic on the house."

Michael glanced up to see the woman as she slid into the seat across from him so they could be eye to eye. He didn't acknowledge her sitting down, picked up the glass, and took a drink instead. It was poorly so mixed he was bombarded by a mouthful of almost nothing but gin. He nearly coughed from the sheer surprise alone but managed to hold off, swallowing the mouthful before setting the glass back down.

Michael cleared his throat before quietly muttering, "Thanks."

"I'm Angelica, by the way."

He shot her a confused look, to which she responded, "I didn't tell you my name yet. So, I thought now would be as good a time as any."

Michael let out an audible sigh before saying, "Just because you bought me a drink it doesn't mean we're going to be friends now." He picked up the gin and tonic. "This was to make up for the drink you made me spill; that's all. You can go now."

The two sat in silence for an elongated and tense moment before Angelica leaned forward to say in a voice just above a whisper, "I know you can hear them."

Michael froze with the glass nearly touching his lips. A flash of panic rolled through him in an instant. He tried to play it off by taking a quick sip, but his evident moment of hesitation had betrayed him. There was no doubt from the look on Angelica's face, she had noticed it.

"They started out as whispers, right?" She relaxed in her seat before continuing, "You probably didn't even notice any black gunk, did you? Not until it latched onto you anyways. That's what happened to me. Before I could understand what was happening the damn stuff squeezed itself up my nose. Of course, that was a couple of years ago, so the voices are a lot louder now. I have to basically get blasted if I want the damn things to turn off."

He stared at her in silence, completely in awe that someone else was dealing with the same thing as him. His brain was overstimulated with amazement to the point he couldn't think clearly. He wanted to ask so many questions, but all that came out was, "How did you know?"

"I've seen it before. I knew a couple of people who went through the same thing. They had the look you have in your eyes. This hopeless...desperate look, like you'd do anything to stop it all."

"What happened to them? The people you knew who heard the voices."

A solemn look came over Angelica's face as she quietly replied, "They died. Every last one of them."

"Oh ... I'm ... I'm sorry," Michael said as he picked up his glass and took a long drink from it. He spent a few moments building up the courage to ask before quickly blurting out, "How did they die?"

"Drinking ... for the most part. One got addicted to other stuff besides the booze. It might have been heroin that finally did her in, but I can't remember. I tend not to think about it."

"That's ... fair." Michael stared down at the ice cubes in his drink for a while until he thought of something else to ask. "How long has this been happening for you?"

"Oh god," Angelica responded as she furrowed her brow to think about it. After a few moments, she answered, "At least four years, maybe closer to five now. Most don't tend to make it this long … so it gets lonely. It's been at least a couple of months since there was someone else I could talk to."

That's when the realization dawned on Michael; the loneliness was the reason she had gotten him the drink. Angelica hadn't wanted to make up for some slight against him; she just wanted someone, anyone, to talk to. He looked up and caught a glimpse of her eyes, seeing isolation and the pain that goes along with it staring back at him. That loneliness was definitely something he could understand. Sure, he had only endured it for a year, but that was more than enough time to feel the sting of seclusion. Perhaps it would be a good thing if he stuck close to Angelica. It certainly wouldn't hurt considering if left alone, he would think about nothing but his mom. He needed some emotional support, and even if she wasn't the greatest of influences, maybe Angelica could work.

"If you're in the same boat as me … then I assume you come here fairly often."

Angelica raised an eyebrow as she replied, "You mean Sam's? Sure. I think I'm in here at least once a week, but

I've got other places I hit up more. I'm more of a whiskey gal, and this place just doesn't do that right."

Michael decided to take a gamble and put himself out there. He took in a deep breath before tentatively saying, "Well … since you've dealt with this … thing a lot longer than I have, I do want to talk some more with you about it. Maybe we could meet back here sometime this week?"

Angelica let out a little laugh. "Slow down there, partner. I don't even know your name."

"It's Michael."

"Nice to meet you, Michael. I guess I'm all right with meeting up here in a few days. However, I'm not going anywhere right now."

Michael quickly downed the rest of his drink before slowly standing to his feet. "You'll be needing a drink then."

Angelica stared at him for a few moments before a brief smile formed as she said, "Maybe an old-fashioned. I doubt they'll get it right, but maybe they will this time."

Chapter Eight
Thirteen months since infection

Michael glanced up from the computer screen to see Angelica shuffle by the library's front desk. It was clear she was having trouble finding him, as her head was constantly scanning the area around her. He gave a wave with his hand to grab her attention, and she hurried over to have a seat at the open computer terminal next to his.

She leaned over into his space and loudly whispered, "So, what's the deal? This isn't one of our usual spots. Why did you want to meet up here?"

"For research," Michael mumbled.

"Research? On what?"

Michael looked up from the web search he was scrolling through to quietly reply, "On the thing that we're both dealing with." He scooted a little toward her to whisper, "The voices."

"Right," Angelica nodded while leaning back in the chair to the point where it almost tipped over. "You know, I've tried it before."

He gave her a look of skepticism. "Oh really? For how long."

"At least a couple of hours, and I didn't find shit."

"Well ... I think it might take a little longer than a few hours." Michael gestured to the shelves of books behind them. "Maybe you can try looking in there while I do this."

Angelica let out a loud groan. "Dude, come on. That's gonna suck." She sat there, anticipating a response that didn't come. After a minute or so of waiting, she reached into her jacket and removed the flask she had been concealing. She took a few swigs and then moved it directly in front of Michael's face.

"What are you doing?" Michael snapped in a volume just above a whisper. "That could get us kicked out of here! Why the hell did you bring that?"

"Gotta keep the voices at bay, right? I bet they're going off in your head right now."

Michael scowled at her, doing his best to resist the temptation as the whispers ate away at his focus. With an unhappy look still on his face, he snatched the flask away from Angelica and shrunk down in the terminal to hide, taking a large gulp. The liquid moved down his throat, leaving a mild burning sensation that took him by surprise. He stifled a cough with all his might before handing the flask back.

The two sat in silence before Angelica stood up while whispering, "You're welcome."

Michael watched as she made her way past the first row of books, then disappeared from view. He shook his head before turning back to the computer and continuing to scan for some useful information. If he was being honest with himself, he had very little faith that they would find anything, but it didn't hurt to try. The past few weeks he had done nothing but stay out all night getting drunk with Angelica at different bars and sleeping the days away. He needed to at least try to find some way to escape from the unhealthy cycle. Even if he didn't dig up anything, there was some small comfort in being able to say he tried.

Chapter Nine
Thirteen months since infection

THE CUE-BALL FLEW FORTH, striking the eleven slightly off course, causing the white sphere to come into contact with the eight-ball.

"Oh crap!" Angelica shouted at the top of her lungs. There was nothing she could do but watch as the eight-ball rolled forward just enough to drop into the corner left pocket.

"Wahoo!" Michael yelled as he lifted his pool stick above his head in celebration. "I remain undefeated yet again! I cannot be stopped!"

"Yeah, yeah, yeah, it doesn't really count. You only won because I scratched."

"Well, if you do it five times in a row, I think it counts," Michael replied with a giant grin plastered across his face.

"Whatever," Angelica rolled her eyes. "Rack 'em up."

Michael chuckled to himself as he inserted the needed quarters to get another game of pool up and going. He carefully took out each ball, placing them in their designated spots inside the metal triangle on the table.

Angelica took a sip of her Moscow mule and watched for a few moments before saying, "I'm sorry we didn't find anything today."

"I wouldn't say we found nothing ... just not a whole lot. I mean ... at least we know there are other people in the world who've been dealing with the black gunk. Well, they say they have anyways."

"That doesn't sound like much to me if I'm being honest."

Michael shrugged as he fit the last ball into place. "I'll take what I can get at this point. If others have been dealing with this, surely someone's figured out how to beat it."

"I wouldn't hold your breath," she muttered to herself. Angelica stepped up, taking a moment to position herself correctly before breaking. As the balls rolled around the table, a striped one went in. "Looks like I'm stripes for once."

"Maybe that'll change your luck."

She let out a small chuckle while moving around the table, trying to find the easiest shot to take. Eventually, she settled on a ball no more than a few inches from a corner pocket. As Angelica bent down to shoot, she said, "Off topic, but you never told me how you got infected with the gunk."

Michael quickly shot back, "You never told me how you did either."

"It was an ex of mine. He called me out of the blue one day and sounded really scared about something. I didn't want to be around the guy anymore, but something about his voice ... made me worried. So, like an idiot, I went and checked up on the bastard. By the time I got there, he was nearly blackout drunk with a bit of the black gunk dripping from his nose. Curiosity got the better of me, and I got a little too close." She let out a deep sigh. "Before I knew what was happening, that damn stuff was wiggling its way into my head." Angelica finally hit the cue-ball, sinking her targeted ball into the hole. "Your turn to spill your guts. How'd the gunk get you?"

Michael was more than reluctant to answer, but he didn't want to cause any tension between him and Angelica. So, he downed the rest of his mixed drink and then replied, "I found my mom. She was dead. I don't know how long it had been, but by the time I found her ... I wasn't really thinking about when she had died. For some reason, out of all the things to pick up on, I noticed the fucking gunk leaking out of her nose." He paused, taking a moment to keep his composure before adding, "You can guess what happened next."

Angelica sank another ball and then quietly replied, "I can." She turned her focus from the game to Michael. "I'm sorry for your loss."

"Well … it was a while ago, so it doesn't hurt so much anymore," he lied. He didn't know why he said it at that moment. Perhaps it was to make himself seem stronger than he was, or maybe he was trying to hide his vulnerability. Either way, he decided to quickly pivot off the topic of his loss. "I guess we've had our share of losing people we care about."

Angelica let out a half laugh. "You're not wrong about that." She went to line up another shot as she added, "Sometimes I think I see them … my dead friends. When it's the middle of the night and I've gone hard with a bottle of tequila. I'll look over at the open area of my hallway, and I swear I'll see someone standing there."

Michael watched as Angelica missed her target completely, scratching the cue-ball in the process. "That's really creepy."

"It is. Until I turn the light on, and there's nothing there." She gestured to the table, "You're up."

"How … how often does that happen?"

Angelica side-eyed Michael as she picked up her drink. "Maybe once a week at most." She took a quick sip before adding, "Don't worry. I'm pretty sure it's the alcohol and not the gunk. You shouldn't have to deal with it."

Michael took a quick shot, knocking in several balls and ending his turn. "I'm still gonna worry."

"Because there might be a chance you start seeing things?"

"No," he shook his head, "because it makes me worry about you."

Angelica smiled at him; some of the grief and worry that had been stuck on her face from the conversation melted away. "I appreciate the concern," she said just before sinking a difficult shot, "but I can take care of myself, you know."

Michael nodded, "Oh, I know."

He watched for a minute or so as Angelica started clearing all the stripes off the table. After knocking in the third consecutive ball, he picked up his nearly empty glass and tried to get the last few drops of his drink. When he was met by nothing but ice cubes, he gave up and headed toward the bar. The whispers were ever so slightly returning, so it was time for another round.

Chapter Ten
Thirteen months since infection

ANGELICA STUMBLED OVER A crack and bumped into Michael. The two let out a ruckus of laughter as they fumbled their way down the sidewalk. Though there were plenty of streetlights to guide their way, the duo found it difficult to avoid obstacles since they were far more than a little drunk. They were so intoxicated that their skin was numb to the chilly, early March weather. Michael led the way, only a few inches in front of Angelica. After stumbling forward for a good twenty minutes, the two finally reached their goal of Michael's apartment complex.

With a great deal of effort, the duo managed to make their way up three flights of stairs. They came to a stop at a door halfway down a poorly carpeted hall, where Michael struggled for several moments before pulling his keys out. He was barely able to keep his hands steady enough to fit the key into the deadbolt, but with a few attempts, he managed it. The door to his apartment let out a loud creak as he lazily pushed it open. Darkness awaited them, but that didn't stop the two from taking a few tentative steps inside.

Michael searched the wall with his hand for the light switch while saying, "Welcome to my humble castle."

His fingers found the plastic protruding from the wall and he flipped it. The lights lit up the living room/kitchen area, and Michael gestured at the newly illuminated space devoid of anything except for a small, beat-up couch and a minuscule TV placed on a worn-out piece of shelving. He waited for Angelica to say something, but she just scanned the room in silence. After an uncomfortably long stretch without sound, she finally wandered over and plopped down on the couch.

"You really don't have much furniture," she commented while letting out a fit of giggles.

Michael rolled his eyes as he retorted, "Oh, like you have so much more than me."

"How would you know? You've never been to my place. For your information, I've got loads of furniture."

"Oh, really?" Michael laughed as he headed into the kitchen. "Loads, you say?"

"Yup! I've got two couches," Angelica announced proudly. "And you know ... my TV is at least ten inches bigger than yours."

"Then I guess we're going to your place next time," he said while searching through his barren cabinets for some booze.

"Next time!" Angelica exclaimed. "Who said there was going to be a next time?"

"Oh, come on. We both know you can't resist me."

Angelica burst out laughing, "Sure. Or maybe I just keep you around for the free drinks."

Michael opened his final set of cabinets, spotting a half bottle of coconut rum. A huge smile spread across his face as he carried the liquor into the living room. He held up the rum. "Well if you're only in it for the free drinks, I better keep them coming then."

Angelica motioned for him to hand over the bottle, eagerly snatching it up when it was close enough. "You're a real-life Romeo," she sarcastically said as she twisted off the cap. She tilted the bottle up to her lips, letting the rum run over her tongue and down the back of her throat.

Michael plopped down just as Angelica finished drinking, causing her to spill some of the liquor on her shirt. She didn't seem to notice and wordlessly handed him the bottle with a smile still on her face. He didn't attack the rum as hard as Angelica did, but he gulped down at least a couple of ounces before resting the bottle on his lap. They sat in silence, with him staring absent-mindedly at the blank TV. He was so accustomed to the noise that constantly pestered his mind that he didn't even pick up on the lack of voices swarming his brain for several minutes. Once he realized the whispers were silent for the moment, a warm, pleasant feeling settled over him.

The combination of alcohol and pleasing sensations brought him to say out loud, "I haven't felt this good in a long time."

"Oh, really? You like the rum that much?"

"I'm not talking about the rum," Michael giggled. "It's just been so long since I've had someone to talk to. The whispers were taking their toll ... but it's been nice having you around. It's a lot easier to deal with this when you're here."

Angelica stared for a moment before slowly smiling. "Yeah, I feel the same way."

She placed a hand on Michael's thigh, and his heart immediately started to race. His adrenaline picked up, just as it had so many times before when the whispers started to attack his mind. Yet, this time was completely different. There was no feeling of anxiety or overwhelming woe. Instead, the pleasant sensation of anticipation flowed through him. In return, he cracked a smile of his own while staring into her brown eyes that he somehow hadn't noticed until then.

"You have really beautiful eyes," he commented.

In response, Angelica slowly raised a hand and gently placed it on his left cheek. It took a mere second for her to lean forward and give him a long and passionate kiss. After a moment, she pulled back with a concerned look on her face since he had just sat there, contributing nothing to the moment. As if reading her mind, he leaned in to meet her lips, and the two kept kissing one another. At some point, she ended up on top of him and they continued their make-out session.

Several more minutes flew by before Michael got up the courage to attempt to say something. He pulled back just enough so he could speak, and in the smoothest voice he could muster, he said, "You know ... I have a bed that might be a little more comfortable. If ... you want to continue this in there."

In response to his offer, Angelica silently pulled herself off the couch before holding out a hand for Michael to take. Once he was standing, he led her to the bedroom, not bothering to turn on the light as they both laid down.

Chapter Eleven

Thirteen to seventeen months since infection

THE MOMENT MICHAEL OPENED his eyes after the wonderful night before, he felt like nothing could touch him. To his surprise, the whispers didn't immediately assault him, allowing him to roll out of bed unimpeded. In fact, he was able to brush his teeth and make breakfast for Angelica before the first mutterings sounded in his mind. That was enough of a respite for him to know he had made the right decision by going from simple drinking buddies with Angelica to something so much more. As they sat there eating their breakfast, he would steal glances at her, getting a warm, bubbling feeling each time he did. He felt like he was on a new kind of high but had been able to achieve it without taking anything.

So, when Angelica asked him, "Where're we drinking tonight?" reality came crashing down on him like a ton of bricks.

They both were still victims of the horrific black gunk; they were still fairly poor since they couldn't hold down mentally taxing jobs, and they still needed to drink to quiet the voices. He knew that was the way things were, but for the first time in over a year, he didn't want to drink. Michael wanted to sit there with Angelica. He didn't care what they did. They could play some stupid board games, or hell, even stare at the wall for several hours. As long as they were together, and as long as they weren't drinking, he would be happy. But that wasn't going to happen, and he knew it. He could tell from the look in her eyes that Angelica was going to be drinking with or without him, and he wanted to be with her more than anything else in the world.

That's why he responded to her question with a reluctant, "It ... it doesn't matter to me."

She clearly didn't pick up on the hesitancy in his voice because she started rattling off a long list of bars. The fact that she was oblivious to how he actually felt hurt Michael. He didn't say anything, choosing to let his emotions stay hidden inside. At the same time, the whispers made themselves known in his head. They quickly grew in volume as the warm, fuzzy feelings he had experienced over the course of the morning died away. Despite his wishes to avoid doing so, he went out with her that night. It took a few drinks, but he finally loosened up enough to enjoy his time with Angelica, and the evening ended with them venturing back to his place again.

This cycle continued over the next few weeks; the days all progressed in the same way. Michael would wake up first and make breakfast, then Angelica would suggest places to drink. With some reluctance, he would go with her and spend the first few hours wishing they had just stayed home. He would nurse the first couple of beverages of the night, while she downed a potent combo of shots and mixed drinks. The sheer amount she went through in such a short time always worried him. Once the alcohol kicked in though, he became too drunk to care and spent the rest of the night enjoying the lack of voices plaguing his brain. Of course, the day always ended with them sleeping together, whether it be at his place or hers.

Through all that time, a nagging sensation ate away at Michael. He kept getting the feeling that if he didn't at the very least, slow down Angelica's drinking, something bad was going to happen to her. The last thing he wanted was for her liver or some other part of her body to fail from the insane amount of liquor she was ingesting, so he kept trying to convince Angelica to slow down. At first, it was with subtle hints, like suggesting beers instead of shots or offering to buy a round and then getting a drink that had to be consumed slowly. When none of that worked, he became far more aggressive with his efforts, eventually reaching the point where he tried to physically drag her out of the bar (which certainly did not work).

His pleading and tactics did nothing to keep her from slamming back shot after shot each night. Bearing witness to the slow demise of someone he cared about was a familiar sight for Michael, and it stung him far worse the second time around. At least when he was a child, he could pretend his mother was okay, but as a grown man, he couldn't do the same with Angelica. It was all too evident from the shakes and near-constant sweating what was happening to her, and it stung not being able to stop the whole thing.

With each passing night, Michael grew more depressed as he watched Angelica downing copious amounts of alcohol. Most of the time he would be sitting in a booth quietly sipping a few drinks, trying only to have enough to keep the voices at bay. Yet the whispers seemed to get stronger, forcing him to down more than the night prior. Regardless of how hard he tried, each night ended with him nearly unable to walk, struggling to move with Angelica as they stumbled toward one of their places. By the time they got inside, he was barely able to comprehend what was happening.

All the while, his concern for Angelica's health grew as more of the same symptoms that had plagued his mom started affecting her. Bouts of intense vomiting seemed to become the norm for her, along with a clear increase in anxiety. She would randomly scream out in her sleep, with the instances becoming more and more frequent. Yet, more troubling than all of that, Michael noticed she was beginning to shake when sober. Her arms or a leg would just start trembling with Angelica completely oblivious to it. These troubling signs were quickly escalating, and even while absolutely plastered, he kept worrying about her health. Eventually, one night, after they were tucked into bed, he couldn't hold his fears in any longer.

"I'm scared," he whispered.

"Huh? Of what?" Angelica had murmured while only half conscious.

"Of all the drinking. I'm scared it's finally catching up with you. I'm terrified that you're suddenly going to die on me."

"Don't worry, baby. That's not going to happen. I'm doing fine."

"That's what my mom used to say ..."

"But I'm not your mom," Angelica quickly replied. "Trust me, I'm totally fine. I would know if I was going too hard. This is just to keep those damn voices away. Everything is going to be okay."

"Yeah?"

"Yeah. Now go to sleep."

Despite what his instincts told him, Michael chose to believe her words. Deep down, he knew that Angelica was not doing okay, but he decided to trust her. Ultimately, in that moment, he wanted to be calmed more than anything else. So instead of continuing to talk to her, he closed his eyes and drifted off to sleep.

<hr>

Michael gradually moved toward consciousness, not due to the sunlight shining in his eyes like he was used to but because of an unpleasant stench. It was a rotten odor that bombarded his nostrils and the second he opened his eyes, he gagged. He had never smelt something so potent before. The stench seemed to be the amalgamation of several different odors. There were fractions of identifiable smells that he noticed seeping out, but he couldn't get a handle on them due to the sheer power of the fetor filling the room.

"Oh god! What the hell is that?" he managed to get out in between gags as he plugged his nose. He turned toward Angelica's side of the bed while asking, "How can you sleep with …"

The unnaturally pale color of her skin stopped him dead in his tracks. An ocean of dread hit him full force as he stared at her chest, desperately hoping for some kind of movement. After a few seconds of watching, he couldn't take it anymore. He grabbed hold of her by the shoulders and shook Angelica, clinging to the smallest bit of hope that she would open her eyes. Unfortunately, all his efforts did was shake loose some of the dried chunks of vomit stuck on her face. Michael ignored the bits of puke that landed on him and continued his desperate attempt to wake his love. When that didn't work, he tried giving her CPR, though he had no idea how to perform it properly. The taste of vomit greeted him when he brought his mouth to hers. He blew air into Angelica's open mouth as hard as he could; his attempts had no effect.

Eventually, he pulled back from Angelica, the adrenaline that had been flowing through him slowly fading. The shock of the discovery diminished, and despair quickly took its place. Tears welled up in Michael's eyes as he sat there, staring at the fresh body before him. He cried as the final words Angelica had spoken to him sounded in his mind. He cried harder than after his mom had died. His sobs shook his body while he curled into a ball only a few inches from Angelica's lifeless body.

"I-I l-love y-you," he choked out before another wave of despair caused him to bawl even harder. "Please don't go!" he cried out over and over, getting louder each time.

Chapter Twelve
Eighteen months since infection

The suit felt a little tight around his stomach as he climbed the concrete steps to the front doors of the church. For a hundred bucks more he could have sprung for something that fit him better, but Michael didn't have that kind of cash. He had almost burned through all the money from his mom's life insurance. The small amount that remained was for alcohol, to keep the damn voices at bay; though, that grew progressively harder to do. They had become so much stronger since Angelica had passed, and it took him twice as many drinks to keep them under control.

Thankfully, the voices had gone down easy this morning, and it seemed like he would be able to pay his final respects. Michael paused for a moment at the church door, his gut twisted in anxious knots. He steadied himself and gently pushed inside. The sanctuary was fairly large, with stained-glass windows lining the walls. There were dozens of pews, with only the first couple of rows full of grieving people. Despite the abundance of open places, he decided to sit in the back, ducking into the very last pew.

He checked the time and noticed there were a few minutes left before the service. As his focus drifted up to the front of the church, he spotted the black casket, closed with no way to see Angelica's body. Michael kept his gaze focused on the coffin, even though there wasn't anything to see. His attention didn't leave the black box until he caught movement heading toward him. He turned his focus to discover what was happening and found himself staring back at an older gentleman with a furious look in his eyes. It was clear that whoever he was, the man was not happy to see Michael there. The intensity of the death glare, combined with the speed at which the guy was walking, intimidated Michael enough for him to stand up.

"Hey, you!" the man snapped as he came within twenty feet of Michael.

That was enough to get Michael to scramble his way out of the pew and head for the exit of the sanctuary. He kept the pace of a fast walk, even though he could feel the angry gentlemen trying to gain ground on him. It was a tense couple of moments before he reached the front doors of the church and opened them up. He headed down the first few steps until a sudden thought crossed his mind. Why was he the one being chased out of the funeral of the woman he loved? No one had the right to do that to him. So, he turned to stand his ground as the man stepped outside, still wearing a death glare.

"You piece of shit!" the older guy shouted.

Anger crept up inside of Michael, and he matched the man's tone as he shouted back, "What the hell is your problem?"

"My problem? My problem is you, you worthless drunk!"

Michael was taken off-guard by the insult. He tried to figure out how it could be that this pissed-off stranger knew he drank. His contemplation didn't last long because the man started to charge down the stairs toward him. Instinctively, he raised his fists, ready to deck the guy if he tried anything. The man stopped short, just a step or two away from him, close enough for Michael to stare into the stranger's eyes. He noticed the fury swirling around the man's pupils, but he also noticed pain and emotional agony mixing with it.

"You've got some pretty big balls coming here," the guy spat out in a wavering tone.

Hurt leaked out with every spoken word, and Michael could tell the man before him was grieving. The doors to the church opened and an older woman came running out. She stopped at the top of the steps and stared down at the two of them.

After a long moment of silence, she spoke in a pleading tone, "Don't do this, Ronaldo. Not here. Not like this."

"He shouldn't be here!" Ronaldo responded while pointing a finger directly at Michael. He glared at him as he seethed with rage. "You killed our Angelica, and then you have the gall to show up here with the rest of us. You don't get to mourn her! We do. You don't!"

"I didn't kill her!" Michael shouted back as he clenched his fists.

"Did you stop her? Huh?" A long pause of silence fell over the scene before Ronaldo scoffed, "That's what I thought."

"I tried to …"

"You tried? How exactly did you try? Did you take her to rehab? Did you have an intervention?" Ronaldo descended the steps so that he was right in Michael's face. He leaned in close and whispered in a wavering voice, "Did you even try to take the damn stuff away from her? Did you even talk to her about it?"

Shame wrapped its ugly grip around Michael, leaving him speechless as Ronaldo stepped back to look him in the eye. Sure, the old man had no idea what Angelica and Michael had been going through, but he was right. He hadn't done nearly enough to stop her from drinking. Hell, there had been only a handful of times he had even suggested not going to a bar, and all of those came with the compromise of stocking up on liquor from the store. As he stood there in front of the grieving parents, a self-loathing thought entered his mind for the first time. What if he hadn't been so afraid to lose her? What if he had just told her how he felt about the drinking, instead of desperately wanting to cling to her? Would it have made a difference? Would that have gotten through to her better than trying to drag her out of the bar? He would never get the chance to know, of course. It was far too late for that.

In the silence, Ronaldo slowly turned and began to climb back up the concrete steps of the church.

Michael couldn't think of anything in the moment except to quietly mutter, "I'm sorry."

This was enough to get Ronaldo to stop and turn his head back to face Michael.

"I'm sorry," Michael barely managed to stutter out.

"No, you're not," Ronaldo bluntly responded. "I've just shamed you enough that you finally feel bad for what you did … but that doesn't mean you're sorry. I can smell it on your breath, you know. After all that damn stuff did to Angelica, you didn't learn to stop drinking it." He paused to take in a shaky breath before continuing, "It hurts. Losing our only daughter hurts … but somehow … knowing that the person who killed her didn't learn a damn thing from her death hurts worse."

"I didn't … it's not like … "

"Please, no more excuses," Angelica's mother said from the top of the steps.

Ronaldo ascended the last of the stairs and came to stand by his wife. "We don't need excuses today. We just want to mourn our daughter in peace and forget that you even exist. So do us a favor and get out of here. Don't come back inside. Because if I see you in there … I will rip your throat out with my bare hands."

With that, the grieving couple turned away from Michael and silently reentered the church, leaving him outside by himself. He stood there for a long time, letting the old man's words flow through his mind. The flask hidden in his inside breast pocket felt heavier with each passing moment. Perhaps it was the shame, or maybe he just realized that he couldn't keep doing this. Either way, Michael made a promise to himself right then and there to stop the drinking while at the same time, vowing to finally silence the voices in his head.

Chapter Thirteen
Eighteen months since infection

THE FIRST SIX OR so hours weren't so bad. Sure, the whispers grew in volume to the point where it felt like there were dozens of regular conversations going on inside his mind at once, but at least his body seemed fine. There were no negative physical side effects to speak of, and he actually felt better. Usually, Michael felt bloated while almost always being hungry at the same time, but the detox gave him a reprieve from these contradictory sensations. With nothing but the voices to focus on, locked away by himself in his apartment, the situation seemed manageable.

For the first couple of hours, he simply sat and binge-watched several shows that had been in his queue for some time, mostly because he had spent the past year and a half too busy drinking from whatever bottle he could find. Of course, the voices tried their hardest to keep Michael from enjoying anything. In response to the whispers, he would turn up the shows bit by bit. Eventually, he maxed out the TV, reaching a point where the volume was hurting his ears. Those efforts only caused him pain as the whispers were unimpeded by the loud noises.

As time slowly drifted by, Michael began to pace about his apartment. Desperate for any remedy to combat the growing conversations in his brain, he started doing body exercises. He only managed to get through a few push-ups and sit-ups before his out-of-shape muscles groaned in pain, causing him to stop. Ultimately, it wouldn't have mattered if he could have continued exercising because shortly after stopping, nausea began to set in. It was slight at first, but the pain in his gut increased over the course of an hour. Growing in intensity, it reached the point where he had to grab his stomach while bending his head toward the ground for any kind of relief.

Things only escalated from there, with sharp and intense headaches adding to his mounting agony. Anxiety also reared its ugly head, as he started to feel overwhelmed by the afflictions that were plaguing him. Eventually, he broke out in a cold sweat, with each bead of the salty liquid feeling like a patch of ice on his skin. Michael writhed in agony on his worn-out couch, trying to push through the simultaneous attacks of nausea and headaches. All the while, the whispers grew louder, reaching the volume of a normal voice, something they had never done before.

Eventually, the nausea culminated in a sudden crescendo, and he felt a wave of unpleasantness roar up from his stomach. He barely had time to roll himself so that his head was hanging off the couch before a round of bile came spewing out onto the floor. There was no doubt that the disgusting multicolored mess would stain the carpet, but that was the least of Michael's worries. He took a shaky hand and wiped his lips while inhaling and exhaling large gasps of air. Mere moments passed before another wave of vomit forced its way out of his body, landing in roughly the same spot as the first glob of puke.

He tried to get up to alleviate some of the pain in his stomach, but another round of vomit came surging forth. The horrific taste brought water to his eyes while the agony that was twisting his gut further added to his misery. Michael tried to beg for mercy from some higher power but it didn't stop more of the puke from rocketing up his esophagus. He barely managed to get a few breaths in between the waves of bile leaving his mouth. By the time the sixth splattering of vomit hit the floor, there was nothing solid left in his stomach. It was obvious to see that now he was puking up stomach acid mixed with whatever liquids had remained in his gut.

"Please," he weakly gasped, "please stop."

Pungent liquid dripped from his lips as he let out a series of pathetic whimpers. All the vomiting had taken away his strength. Most of his energy had been expended, so he could do nothing except lie there. Thanks to his inability to move, he was subjected to the view of his puke lying on the carpet. His nostrils hovered directly over the disgusting glop, so he had no choice but to smell the horrific odor that rose into the air. For several minutes he lay there, trying to calm down and stop his body from trembling. Eventually, he built up enough strength to wipe some of the chunky spittle from his lips, which only worked to transfer the grotesque substance to the back of his hand. He was far too tired to wash himself off, so he just laid there on the couch until his exhaustion drove him to close his eyes. Sleep came quickly, and with it, a respite from the never-ending cacophony of voices.

Chapter Fourteen
Eighteen months since infection

THE FIRST THING TO greet Michael's eyes when he awoke was the now-dried pile of his vomit. Thanks to the faint glow of the yellow light coming from the lamppost in the parking lot of his apartment complex, he could faintly make out the chunks of partially digested food sticking out from the carpet. Though it had dried, the bile still produced an awful odor, which gave Michael the drive to finally pull himself off the couch. As he got to his feet, he let out a series of coughs that tore at his dry throat. Immediately, he made his way to the kitchen where he chugged several glasses of lukewarm tap water.

After sucking down his fourth refill, the whispers once again began their assault on Michael's mind. The jumble of dozens of voices speaking at once immediately got on his nerves. He gulped down a tad more of the passable water, doing his best to ignore the whispers. However, the voices succeeded at getting under his skin thanks to his already bad mood from the grueling detox. Quickly, his temper rose, with each individual voice irritating him as a mosquito bite would. The poking and prodding of his brain seemed so much more annoying than usual, and his emotions took hold.

Anger rose above all other feelings and Michael yelled at the top of his lungs, "What the hell do you want, huh? What the hell do you want from me?"

Of course, he didn't anticipate a coherent reply. Over the months that the voices had tormented him, Michael hadn't been able to understand what they were saying once. So, he was taken by surprise when all whispers faded away but one. This single, raspy whisper responded to his question with one word, *look.*

He instantly knew what the voice meant, but he tried to convince himself that he didn't. Michael stood in the kitchen, using all his willpower to stay still, all while his curiosity drifted part of his focus elsewhere. When he didn't budge, another whisper joined the first in chanting that one word. Their tone shifted from a simple answer to more of a command as additional voices joined in. He wanted to deny them, but he was intrigued as to what they wanted him to see. More than likely, there would be nothing waiting for him, but the curiosity was overwhelming.

The voices raised their chanting as he cautiously advanced to the area where the second-rate laminate of the kitchen transformed into carpet. He held himself on that precipice in hesitation for a long moment before finally taking his first steps forward. Michael scanned the living room, spotting nothing out of the ordinary as he did so. Eventually, his gaze came to rest on the entrance of the hallway, which was almost completely shrouded in darkness. After a few seconds of staring, the voices dissipated in volume, their chant becoming less intensive. He got the message and continued to gaze at the darkness roughly twenty feet in front of him, anxiously waiting to see if something would happen.

It took his eyes a while to adjust, but as they gradually did, he noticed there was an unfamiliar shape in the hall. Whatever the strange object was, Michael could tell that it had to be at least five feet in height. As he intently stared at the foreign shape trying to ascertain what it was, the thing moved. It was the tiniest shift, but it was enough that he noticed. A sharp jolt of terror ripped through him as several different possible answers for what the object could be flashed through his mind; none of them were good. Tense moments dragged by before the next sign of movement, this time far clearer than the last.

Fear took over his vocal cords, and he squeaked out, "Stop!"

The apparition froze, seemingly obeying his pathetic request, but after a few seconds, it moved once again. Mere moments passed before the thing reached the end of the hall, coming to a stop as if some invisible barrier kept it from progressing into the living room. This gave Michael a chance to get a look at it. However, the thing was still covered in shadow, so he was unable to make out any true details. Nevertheless, he could see its shape and he easily identified it as a woman's figure. Some of the frightful options that had filled his mind were eliminated with the discovery, but this did not do much to assuage his terror. His dread was so great that he remained locked, frozen in place as the figure finally took a single step forward.

"Stop!" he yelled in utter panic. "Don't come any closer! I swear ... if you do ..."

His threat was ignored as the figure took another step, completely emerging into the living room. Though the faint light from the parking lot fell over the shape, it was still covered in darkness, making it seem as though the figure was crafted in shadow. Michael's heart thumped inside his chest, fueled by the adrenaline that was being wasted by him standing still. Cold sweat poured down his cheeks while the figure took a couple more steps, coming within a few feet of him. Though it was nearly at arm's length, the shape continued to be covered in impenetrable blackness. Despite not being able to make out any details, there was something familiar about the figure, but his mind was too terrified to recognize what. The apparition took one last step, coming to a stop mere inches from him, where it just stood there letting out low and heavy breaths.

Michael's whole body shook with fear as his eyes stared at the strange being before him. Tension filled the air as he waited for the shape to do something, but it continued to remain motionless. Finally, he built up the courage to ask in a meek whisper, "W-What a-are you?"

The figure stopped breathing and a long silence followed, before in a ragged and inhuman voice, it responded, *you don't recognize your own mother?*

"What? What did you say? How ... what is this?" Michael started to ramble as his brain desperately tried to comprehend what the thing had just said.

He began to feel faint, his mind completely overwhelmed by the unprecedented situation he found himself in. Michael felt nauseous, but it was a completely different sensation from when he had vomited a few hours prior. The room started to spin around him while his mind slowed itself down, desperately trying to defend itself. In the blink of an eye, he had fallen to the floor, exhausted once more. The figure claiming to be his mother looked down at him as he drifted out of consciousness.

CHAPTER FIFTEEN
Eighteen months since infection

THE MOMENT HIS EYES opened, Michael bolted upright, widely scanning the area around him for the unnatural figure. He didn't find anything on his first sweep, but he continued looking until he was certain nothing was lurking somewhere in the dark. Gradually, his gaze drifted to the window looking out at the parking lot. Slowly, he got to his feet and moved over to peer down at the ground below. He had no way of knowing how long he had been asleep, but clearly, it was still dark out. In the best-case scenario, he had only been unconscious for a few hours, though there was a possibility that he slept through an entire day.

Regardless of how long he had been out, Michael still felt awful and off balance. His clothes were damp with what he hoped was sweat while an unpleasant sensation continued to linger in his gut. He turned and glanced down at the dried pile of vomit; his gaze held on it as he replayed the last few minutes before he lost consciousness. While he sifted through every little detail in his mind, the first of the whispers returned. Though it was on its own, he couldn't understand any of what the voice was trying to say. Slowly, the whisper's words became more pronounced just as another joined in.

Due to the unreal encounter he had gone through with the figure shrouded in darkness, Michael felt drained both physically and emotionally. Instead of feeling anger and annoyance toward the growing whispers, he experienced despair. All he hoped for in the moment was a reprieve from it all, and not just the voices. He was tired of the pain, the grief, and, of course, the loneliness. The guilt eating away at him had become an unbearable burden that he simply wanted to end. So, as the whispers grew into a cacophony of incomprehensible babbles, he made his way to the kitchen. He searched for a few seconds through the drawers before pulling out a single steak knife. Held in his right hand, he stared down at the sharp blade as he contemplated whether to use it or not.

The voices made their opinion on the matter known, as they joined in unison to constantly chant, *do it.*

He continued to stare at the knife while softly asking, "What do you get out of this? Why do you want me to do this?"

We get nothing.

Michael continued to hesitate as his mind tallied the pros and cons of going through with it. Dozens of memories cycled through his brain, with most of them being unpleasant. He thought of his mom and Angelica, lingering on the love he had lost. Suddenly, his thoughts pivoted to the uncomfortable confrontation he had gone through with Angelica's father. Specifically, he played one thing over and over again. "It hurts. Losing our only daughter hurts ... but somehow ... knowing that the person who killed her didn't learn a damn thing from her death hurts worse."

Slowly, inch by inch, he lowered the knife until he laid it down on the kitchen counter. He realized that going through with it would be an insult to Angelica. She wouldn't have wanted him to just give up. She would have pushed for him to fight, to keep going. Taking a shortcut to escape the pain would mean her death had truly been in vain, and he wasn't going to let that happen.

NO! The voices suddenly screamed, reaching a volume far louder than they ever had before. Michael felt a sharp pain stab his brain, and he instinctively grabbed the sides of his head. The voices continued to scream in protest, but instead of Michael picking up the knife, he stumbled backward, colliding with his fridge. He groaned in agony while pushing himself out of the kitchen, putting further distance from what the voices wanted him to do.

Do it! You know you want to! Just do it! The pain will go away! It's what you deserve after letting Angelica die.

Suddenly, Michael caught movement out of the corner of his eye. He pivoted his focus just in time to witness someone race out of the hallway. Before he could react, the person leapt toward him. Taken by surprise, he tried to back-peddle but ended up tripping over his own feet and tumbling to the floor. The intruder took advantage and threw themself on top of him, allowing Michael to get a good look at his attacker. He stared in complete shock as his assailant, Angelica, looked down at him. Except, it wasn't Angelica; there was something off about her. All her features were twisted and warped so that she resembled Angelica while looking nothing like her at the same time.

The fake Angelica began to rain down a series of blows upon Michael who only responded with defense. He held up his arms as a shield and allowed the hits to connect with his limbs while he tried to comprehend what was happening.

You killed me! The fake Angelica screamed in between blows.

"No!" Michael shouted in protest. "I didn't kill you; the voices did! The alcohol did! I wanted to save you. I tried to save you!"

But you didn't! You let me die because you're weak. You're pathetic!

Michael focused all his energy into his legs, and with a quick push against the floor, he was able to throw the fake Angelica off him. Quickly, he scrambled to his feet, ready for another attack, but there was no sign of her. In his confusion, he didn't realize something was behind him until the twisted replica of his dead mother landed a punch on his right side. He grabbed the spot in pain while spinning around just in time to block the next punch. Only a few seconds later, the fake Angelica reentered the fray, and the two revenants wailed away on Michael.

Being attacked from the front and the back was too much for him to handle, and he desperately tried to retreat, but the mutated women followed him step after step. Each attack that landed was more painful than the last, and Michael could feel his body start to fold from the damage. In a last-ditch effort, he widely swung his fist at his faux mother but didn't manage to connect. The blows continued until he finally dropped to his knees, covering his face with his arms as a final defense. Even on the floor, the two specters didn't let up, continuing to assail him at full force.

Weak! Worthless! Pathetic!

Pain radiated from almost every inch of his body while the verbal abuse slowly chipped away at his psyche. He tried wildly swinging one of his arms, hoping to hit something, but it just didn't work. There was nothing he could do except protect himself as much as possible and hope that the beating didn't kill him. He tried to block out the insults, but that only made him focus on the pain more. The physical agony was too much, and he allowed the insults to hurt him.

This unrelenting abuse continued until his faux mother sneered, *I should have never had you. My life would have been so much better if you wouldn't have been born.*

Something inside him snapped at those words and fury flowed through his veins. Despite the blows, he pulled himself to his feet. Adrenaline rushed through his body, making him almost completely numb to the attacks. With the pain dulled, he was able to move and react, delivering a punch that hit the fake Angelica directly in the face. As the injured specter stumbled back, Michael attacked his faux mother, landing a series of blows that knocked it off its feet.

"You're not my mom!" he yelled at the top of his lungs. "She may not have been the best mother in the world, but she loved me more than anything else. There's no way she would ever say something like what you did. Never!"

The twisted visage of his fake mom stared up at Michael in shock as he advanced on her. His anger flowed through into his fists, and he mercilessly delivered punch after punch. He was only interrupted when he felt a sharp pain in his lower back. Turning around, he found that the fake Angelica had landed a blow. In response, he turned his aggression toward her, furiously slamming his fists into her warped body. He continued his barrage until the twisted shape fell to the floor, where it seemed as though the thing pretending to be Angelica would stay.

Michael turned his attention back to his fake mother, "You're not my mom ... and she's not Angelica. You're both just a trick, conjured up by the black gunk inside my head. I doubt you're even here."

In an instant, the two assailants disappeared, leaving Michael alone in the silence that hung over his apartment. A small bubbling sense of hope started to form as he felt like the whole ordeal was finally over. However, that proved to be naïve as the voices came roaring inside his mind at full force. Their overpowering shrieks tore at his mind, sending ripples of pain throughout his body.

Reeling from the agony, he blindly stumbled around the living room while screaming for relief.

We know what you want, so just do it. It'll be over quickly then the pain will be gone. No more hurt, no more fear. It's what you want. We know what you want. You want…

"I want my mom back, you fuckers!" Michael screamed at the top of his lungs. "I want Angelica back! I need them back!"

Grief surged forth from inside him, overpowering all his other senses. Tears began to form at the corners of his eyes while he collapsed onto the floor and the voices momentarily stopped attacking him. He sat there sobbing, truly grieving all that he had lost for the first time in over a year. Michael allowed himself to feel each tear, each painful memory, and that made him weep even more.

"I just want them back," he managed to whimper out through his sobs, "but that's not possible. You can't bring them back, can you?"

No, we can't.

"Then I'll make sure you don't get anything you want."

Do you think you can stop us? Your mother and Angelica couldn't.

"I know I can. After all, you're trapped in my body; you can't do anything that I don't want to do. I'm not your prisoner; you're mine."

We won't just go away! We'll make your life a living hell!

"You already have," he replied as he wiped a bit of snot dripping from his nose. "That was your big mistake. You took everything I loved. Now I have nothing but hate, anger, and the drive to make you suffer. I promise you, from this point on, you will never win."

With that proclamation, the voices went silent, and Michael could finally sit with his emotions. The tears came once more, and he held himself as he bawled harder than he ever had before. "I just want them back," he whispered to himself, "I just want them back."

Chapter Sixteen
Two and a half years since infection

THE GLASS MADE A loud clinking noise as it slammed down on the table. Michael couldn't help but flash a scowl of annoyance at his coworker as the man let out an obnoxiously loud sigh of pleasure. He tried to ignore the guy as he took a sip from his water, which was only slightly above room temperature. As he still had the glass up to his lips, something happened on one of the dozens of TVs in the bar that caused the other patrons to yell out in excitement. Several of his coworkers even jumped up from their seats, with one of them bumping into him. The sudden bump was enough to knock the glass out of Michael's grasp, and he spilled water on his lap.

Much to his growing annoyance, the coworker didn't even apologize for what he had done. As he grabbed a couple of napkins from the center of the table to wipe up the mess, Michael started to wonder why he had even shown up. Sure, his boss had told him it would be good for team-building purposes and to get to know the rest of the people he'd be working alongside, but that didn't seem so important anymore. After a good hour or so in a non-working environment with his peers, he realized he didn't want to get to know any of them. They were all inconsiderate corporate stooges, too focused on their own lives to care about anyone else.

"Hey, Michael."

He glanced up from the wet spot on his pants and made eye contact with his boss sitting on the other end of the table.

"Did you manage to get all that data put together for the coverage report?"

"Almost," Michael reluctantly replied, "there are a few things I still need to get."

"Well, I need it first thing tomorrow morning, so you're probably going to be doing some work tonight."

"Yes, sir," Michael quietly replied with a nod.

A large knot of anxiety formed in his gut as his boss turned his attention back to whatever game was on. Michael knew there was still a good five or six hours of work that needed to be done on the project, which meant his night was completely shot. On top of that, his boss had sprung this arbitrary deadline on him, and he did not like that at all. Anxiety and frustration started to swirl around inside his mind the more he thought about the whole situation. Only a few weeks into the job and he was already reaching a breaking point. As doubt over whether he could get the report done that night started to form, a low whisper reached him.

You could use a drink. With all the hard work you've done this week, you've earned it.

Michael eyed the bar off to his left with a growing want for a strong drink tugging at him. The lone whisper was quickly joined by others, urging him to get himself one. He reached his hand into his left pocket and wrapped his fingers around the metal chip inside. His eyes remained focused on the bar, watching the bartender mix up some type of margarita as he pulled the item from his pocket. He held the metal chip below the table, so no one else could see it but him. As the whispers grew, he glanced down at the symbol of a triangle with a large one in the middle of it to represent a whole year of sobriety. The chip reaffirmed his goals, and the voices faded ever so slightly.

He closed his eyes and focused all his efforts on forcing the whispers into silence. It was a trick he had learned several months ago that he continued to work on perfecting. The exercise took all his mental prowess and left him drained afterward, but it was well worth it. In truth, Michael had realized that the black gunk fed on negative emotions, so his new technique was nothing more than affirming all the positive things in his life. The problem was that the voices fought back, and that was the part that made him weak. Regardless, he gave everything he had at that moment, focusing solely on listing off the positive things happening to him. Even when a sharp pain tore across his brain, he kept his concentration, and the voices faded back into low whispers.

"Michael, are you okay?"

He opened his eyes and quickly answered, "Yeah, I'm fine. I was just doing a little meditation exercise."

"Oh, I wasn't talking about that," the coworker who had gotten his attention gestured at his own nose, "I ... think you've got a nosebleed, man."

Michael grabbed a napkin and lightly dapped it under his nose. Pulling the makeshift tissue away from his face, he immediately spotted the black substance soaking into the napkin. The gunk had fought back a lot harder than he originally thought. A sudden and sharp headache took hold, causing him to wince in pain. He attempted to play it cool, cleaning up the rest of the area around his nose. Trying not to make a scene, he simply left the napkin as he slowly rose to his feet. Even with sobriety and positive life affirmations, Michael had come to terms with the fact that he was fighting a lifelong war against the black gunk, but that didn't make it any less painful when he lost battles against it. Though it had been a small skirmish, with him sitting there silently in the crowded bar, he had lost. The voices had sapped too much of his strength, he needed to get home and rest.

"Well, everybody, I'm gonna head out. I've got some stuff to take care of."

He didn't listen to the round of ingenuine goodbyes as he put on his coat and headed out the door. Halfway across the parking lot, Michael felt a warm liquid start to drip from his nose. With trepidation, he placed a finger under his nose and pulled it away, breathing a sigh of relief when he found blood instead of the black gunk. Despite the mental strain that keeping the voices at bay had taken on him, he could take solace in the fact that he hadn't turned to the bottle to stop it. That was the one victory he could take out of the day, and it was the biggest one for him. So, as he drove out of the parking lot, there was a sense of hope. Sure, he had his never-ending war with alcohol and the black gunk on his mind, but for once, it seemed doable.

Meanwhile, inside the bar, Michael's coworkers continued to drink while they watched the game. As they kept up their cheering, the one who had been sitting on Michael's left went for a napkin, not noticing his arm had brushed against the used one on the table. Only a few minutes later, a busboy came and cleared off a good chunk of the bottles, as well as all the trash, including the napkin with the black gunk on it. Little did the two men know that they had something in common now. They both would soon play host to a parasite that would change their lives for the worse.

Radar DeBoard is just a simple horror writer, living in the bleak state of Kansas. Recently, he has grown weary of the limitations of his craft when it comes to scares. Sure, he has terrified many thanks to having four published books to his name as well as being featured in dozens of horror anthologies, but the fear from those stories wears off. He wishes to create something so horrific that it lingers in the reader's mind for years to come. Creating something of such unfathomable terror would cement him in the brains of those who purchase his books. Plus, it would be like he left a piece of himself in each copy of his work. A small bit of himself that can grow and watch, waiting for the right time to deliver a final fright.